Jumping Mouse

It leaks through my fingers like rain,

The great roaring noise.

Nothing can keep it out,

Not even the denials of my friends.

Jumping Mouse

Retold by Brian Patten
Illustrated by Mary Moore

HAWTHORN PRESS

Jumping Mouse 2nd Edition
Text © Brian Patten 2010
Illustrations and cover image © Mary Moore 2010

Brian Patten is hereby identified as the author of this work in accordance with section 77 of the Copyright, Designs and Patent Act, 1988. He asserts and gives notice of his moral right under this Act.

Published by Hawthorn Press, Hawthorn House,
1 Lansdown Lane, Stroud, Gloucestershire, GL5 1BJ, UK
www.hawthornpress.com

First edition published by George Allen & Unwin Ltd 1972

Cover design by Lucy Guenot
Typeset in Times New Roman by Bookcraft Ltd, Stroud
Printed in China by Everbest Printing Co Ltd

Printed on FSC approved paper

British Library Cataloguing in Publication Data applied for

ISBN 978-1-903458-99-0

For Angela
who introduced me to this tale

Introduction

Roger Ridington, an American anthropologist, told the story of Jumping Mouse to a meeting of the American Anthropological Association over forty years ago in the United States, in order to illustrate a lecture on the American Indians. He went into the story's meaning and suggested the symbolic qualities of the creatures in the tale. The story, a folk tale, was told to him by Chuck Storm (Hyemeyohsts). It was told to me by a friend one evening when we were riding through Dublin on the top deck of a Corporation bus. Stories, like buses, travel...

Here it is retold again, in simple yet I hope clear language that will make the story easily accessible to adults and children alike. Perhaps one of its 'lessons' is that all creatures are part of a whole, that they interact, give to and take from each other no matter how important or insignificant they might at first appear. Another is how we can all grow and fulfill our potential by overcoming fear. Several versions of this story exist. The original author probably told it round campfires centuries ago, and has since entered whatever Heaven he believed in, along with a most amazing and innocent mouse.

Brian Patten

In the roots of a giant tree there once lived a family of mice...

IN the roots of a giant tree there once lived a family of mice. It was a huge family and they lived in semi-darkness, for the tree's thick branches hid the sunlight from them. They went about their business hardly ever venturing out into the world. When the stars appeared they slept, and when the sun tried to light their gloomy home they worked, poking their tiny faces into holes to see if there was anything edible there. They gathered seeds and bits of fluff and twigs, which they moved from one place to another. They were always rushing about.

Among these mice was one who kept hearing a roaring noise. When he asked the others what the noise was they always said, 'It must be your imagination. We can hear no noise.' The more he asked about the noise the more the other mice insisted that no noise existed. The mouse would then go back to his work among the tree-roots. He would try to forget about the noise. But it was difficult. At night he would lie restless on the moss under the tree and look up at the stars through the leaves. The roaring bothered him so much he could not sleep. He wondered what the noise could be. But because he had never been out into the world beyond the tree-roots, he could not begin to imagine what it was.

He tried putting his hands over his ears to shut out the roaring noise. It would not go away. It leaked through his fingers like rain. It leaked into his ears – a beautiful, loud and terrible roaring!

One day he could stand it no longer. He decided he must find out what caused the great roaring. So he crept away from the tree, and while the other mice were scurrying about in the darkness he went out into the world.

In the world beyond the tree-roots the day was hot, and the little mouse had not gone very far when he met a raccoon.

'Hello, Brother Raccoon,' he said.

The raccoon was surprised when he heard the mouse. 'Why, hello Brother Mouse,' he replied. 'What are you doing out here in the world?'

He knew of course about raindrops
and often woke to find them splattering
round him on the moss.

The mouse told him about the noise he could hear and how he had come to find out what it was.

'Why,' said the raccoon, 'that's the Great River you can hear. I go there every day to wash my food.'

The little mouse was delighted. He wasn't imagining things after all! He wanted to go to this river and see exactly what it was. He had never seen a river before.

'Is the Great River like the mountain lions I've heard of?' he asked the raccoon. 'It certainly roars loudly enough.'

'It is nothing at all like a mountain lion,' laughed the raccoon.

The mouse decided he would take a bit of the Great River back home with him to show the other mice. He wanted to prove to them that the roaring noise was real, and that it existed outside his head as well as inside it.

'Do you think whoever owns the river will mind me borrowing a bit of it?' he asked.

'You're a rather naive mouse!' laughed the raccoon. 'No one owns the river. It belongs to us all.'

'You mean there's a special bit that belongs to mice, and a special bit that belongs to raccoons?' asked the mouse.

'It doesn't come in bits,' said the raccoon. 'The bits stop becoming bits when they become the river.'

The mouse was puzzled. 'Will you take me to this river then?' he asked.

'Certainly,' said the raccoon.

When they came to the edge of the river the mouse was amazed. It was such a wonderful sight. He blinked at the bright waters. He had

When they came to the edge of the river the mouse was amazed.

not expected anything so grand or powerful. He knew of course about raindrops, and often woke to find them splattering round him on the moss. And he knew about dew as well, and about puddles left by the rain. But this river! Ten thousand years of dew wouldn't be this grand! Not ten hundred thousand drops of rain, nor all the tears ten thousand mice could ever cry. The river tickled his heart. He went with the raccoon to its edge and, peering over the bank, saw his own reflection.

'For all its roaring the Great River obviously wishes me no harm,' he thought. 'It carries branches and leaves along with it. It is powerful enough to wash away the earth and uproot trees, and yet it allows my reflection to rest upon its surface without being washed away.

It was still early in the morning. The mouse sat sniffing the freshness of the air and watching the bright frost melt from the grass. When he closed his eyes the roaring of the river was loudest. It was a powerful music, and it made his small head dizzy. He sat a long time, and had completely forgotten about the raccoon who was busy washing his food. When the raccoon had finished he came back to the mouse and said: 'I've got to leave, but I'll take you along to see my friend the frog.'

They walked along the river bank, and soon came to where the frog lived. He was a large green frog, and sat half in, half out of the water. 'Hello little brother,' he said when the mouse came towards him.

He was a large green frog, and sat half in, half out of the water.

He was a friendly frog. He told the mouse interesting things about the river, and explained how frogs could live both on land and in the water. 'Most of us begin in one element and move to another,' he said. The frog told the mouse about the huge thunderstorms that happened, and about the lightning that lit up the world for just a second at a time. And about how nice it was to hibernate and to dream throughout the winter, and of how glad and awake he felt when the spring returned.

Then the frog asked: 'Why did you come here?'

'Because of the roaring noise in my ears,' answered the mouse.

'That's a lovely reason,' said the frog, and then he asked the mouse if he wanted a gift.

'Yes', said the mouse, 'I'd like that.' And although the mouse did not know what a gift was, everything seemed so good he was sure he would enjoy it.

'To receive your gift you must jump up as far as you can,' said the frog.

So the mouse did. He crouched down on the river bank until he was a tight little bundle, and then he leapt up into the sky. It was a remarkable jump. He leapt higher than the trees, passing the birds in

And then he leapt up into the sky.

their nests and the squirrels dozing on their branches. Up and up he went and then – splash! Instead of landing back on the river bank, he fell into the water. The mouse was frightened and very nearly drowned. Fortunately the part of the river into which he had fallen was shallow, and he managed to scramble out.

'You tricked me,' said the mouse. 'I'm sure a gift isn't a bit like that.'

The mouse was fond of the frog and was upset that he should have been tricked.

'You're safe, aren't you?' asked the frog.

'Yes,' said the mouse.

'And you aren't really hurt, are you?'

'No,' said the mouse.

'Then what on earth are you complaining about! When you jumped up didn't you see something even more remarkable than the Great River?'

'Yes,' said the mouse, 'I saw the most wonderful mountains.'

'They are the Sacred Mountains,' said the frog, 'and that glimpse of them is my gift to you. And you've also got a name now. From now on you are called Jumping Mouse.'

Jumping Mouse was delighted with his name. He wanted to go back home immediately and tell the rest of the mice about all the things that had happened. 'They'll believe me now,' said Jumping Mouse. 'How can they possibly doubt the roaring noise after these things have happened?' He told the frog he was going back, and the frog said: 'Always keep the roaring noise in your heart and in your ears, that way you will always be able to find the river and won't get lost.'

Jumping Mouse returned to the roots of the giant tree. The other mice were still there in the gloom, moving their seeds from one place to another.

He rushed in among them. His eyes were wild with excitement. He spluttered and told them about the Great River and about all the other wonderful things outside. He begged them to come out and see for themselves, but they did not believe him. They backed away in horror.

Jumping Mouse had quite forgotten about falling into the river. He was covered with leaves, and his fur smelt peculiar. The other mice said, 'He's mad. Its quite obvious that some terrible beast has had him in its mouth. It's a wonder he came back at all.'

They stayed clear of Jumping Mouse. He was miserable amongst them. He wanted to share his excitement, but the others would not listen to him. They pretended to stuff their ears up with seeds and ignored him.

Jumping Mouse decided it was no use staying among the tree-roots any longer. He didn't like to be thought mad when he knew he was quite sane. So he told them he was going back outside to find the Sacred Mountains.

He begged them to come out and see for themselves.

'It's a much better thing to do than moving seeds from one place to another,' he said.

'You're insane,' the mice shouted. 'The Eagles will get you!'

Mice were terrified of eagles. Of all the things in the world they were scared of, it was eagles they feared the most. For eagles considered mice tasty little morsels. Still, no matter how afraid he was, Jumping Mouse decided to go back outside.

'Anything is preferable to staying here,' he said.

He was no longer content to move seeds from one place to another. The world contained too many wonders for him to keep on doing the same thing day after day after day.

He stood at the tip of the shade cast by the tree and looked around him. The raccoon was no longer about, but Jumping Mouse could still hear the roaring noise, and so he followed it back to the river.

He crept through the grass, keeping well hidden. When he reached the river he wandered along the banks in the direction of the Sacred Mountains.

He stood at the tip of the shade cast by the tree and looked around him.

The world was dreamy. There were flowers that burnt with colours he had not noticed before. So different and so much more beautiful was the world outside the tree-roots that Jumping Mouse wandered through it astonished and silent. He found seeds to eat that were big and fat like plums. And he drank from tiny pools of crystal water. When the night fell he made a bed out of turf and grass, and left a little hole through which he could peep out at the stars and keep watch in case there were any eagles about.

He travelled along the river bank for days. He met a million and one creatures. There were small birds and iridescent beetles and various butterflies and bees, all going about their business in the sunlight. 'Hello, Brother,' he would say to them when he was close. 'Hello, Brother Jumping Mouse,' they answered. The world was fresh; it was alive with colours and movement. Among the tree-roots time had passed so quickly and the days had been indistinguishable, linked drearily to each other without change or interruption. But now each moment was filled with some new marvel.

Sometimes he stayed with the creatures he met and he listened to their stories more often than he spoke himself. Other days he would eat early and wander on without meeting a single creature. One night there was a thunderstorm and he remembered what the frog had told him about lightning, and about how the world was lit up for the briefest of moments and then fell back into darkness. He saw it happen. He saw the fruits on trees lit up like tiny suns. He saw each blade of grass in the field leap out, sharp and clear and green. He heard the thunder roll through the sky, roaring louder even than the river.

One day Jumping Mouse came close to a great wilderness across which he had to travel to reach the Sacred Mountains. In a circle of sweet sage he met another mouse. It was an ancient old thing, but Jumping Mouse was glad to have found a friend on the edge of the

'We have been further than any other mice before us.'

wilderness. He told the old mouse about how he had come out to explore. He spoke about the raccoon and the frog, and about how he had jumped up so high he had seen the Sacred Mountains. 'I'm on my way to visit them,' he said.

'I too have heard the roaring noise and been to the River,' said the old mouse. 'But I'm convinced the Sacred Mountains don't exist. I've never seen them. Why not stay here in the sweet-sage patch? After all, we have been further than any other mice before us.'

Jumping Mouse said he did not want to stay in the sweet-sage patch. 'I want to find the Sacred Mountains more than anything,' he said. 'Even more than growing old and wise.'

The old mouse was annoyed. 'The eagles will get you,' he threatened.'Out in the wilderness there is no shelter, and they are bound to see you.'

Jumping Mouse ran to the very edge of the wilderness and hid amongst some shrubs. They were the very last things in which he could shelter. He looked up into the sky, and in the distance he could see the blurry outlines of eagles gliding round in circles looking for food. He was wondering how he could get across the wilderness without being seen

'And nothing can save me but the eye of a mouse'

by them when he heard a groaning noise, a kind of crying, just in front of him. He peeped through the shrubs and saw a huge buffalo stretched out on the ground.

'Hello, Brother Buffalo,' said Jumping Mouse. 'Why are you groaning?'

'Because I'm blind and dying', answered the buffalo, 'and nothing can save me but the eye of a living mouse.'

When he heard this, Jumping Mouse was shocked. The buffalo was a large and impressive creature; he thought it would be a sin to let such a wonderful animal die. He wanted very much for the buffalo to live. Jumping Mouse decided to help. 'If it will make you live you can have one of my eyes,' he said.

As soon as he said this one of his eyes flew from his head and entered into the buffalo. Immediately, the buffalo rose from the ground, quite well again. 'I know who you are now', he said. 'You are Jumping Mouse, and you want to cross the wilderness. I will help you.' The buffalo told Jumping Mouse to hide in the fur on his back.

'That way you will become part of me and be safe.' Jumping Mouse and the buffalo thundered across the wilderness, and soon they arrived on the lower slopes of the Sacred Mountains, where the buffalo said, 'I can go no further.'

Jumping Mouse thanked the buffalo and watched as it thundered back into the wilderness. There was little to shelter Jumping Mouse from the eagles now, only the shadows cast by stones.

When Jumping Mouse looked up at the Sacred Mountains it became evident that he was not going to be able to climb them alone. There were so many paths, and he had no idea which of them to take. He was beginning to think he would never get to the top when a wolf came into view. The wolf was acting rather peculiarly. It was running round in circles, muttering to itself and barking in the strangest manner.

'Hello, Brother Wolf,' said Jumping Mouse.

'Wolf? Am I a wolf?' asked the wolf, still running around. 'I seem to have forgotten what I am and where and how and why, and I feel quite useless.' The wolf looked so confused and dejected that Jumping Mouse felt a great pity for the creature. 'Is there any way I can help you?' he asked.

'Not at all,' replied the wolf. 'I'm going mad and I'm bound to starve. I've forgotten what I eat and eat what I've forgotten. Last night I tried to fly and tomorrow I'll try to swim. I'm bound to drown. Buttercups and lightning are my brothers but mice don't exist.' Jumping Mouse had heard something like this before. 'What do you mean, mice don't exist?'

'It stands to reason and I'm reasonless.'

'Well,' said the wolf, 'only the eye of a mouse can make me sane. So they can't exist. It stands to reason and I'm reasonless.'

Now Jumping Mouse wanted very much to reach the top of the Sacred Mountains. He had come all this way, and he wanted to reach the top more than anything else in the world. Even his sight was not as important to him as the Sacred Mountains. And so although it meant he would be blind, he said to the wolf: 'Mice do exist and I'm a mouse. You can have my eye.'

When he said this his other eye flew out of its socket and entered into the wolf. The wolf immediately came back to his senses, and recognised Jumping Mouse.

'Ah,' said the wolf. 'You are Jumping Mouse and I am to guide you to the top of the Sacred Mountains.'

Jumping Mouse climbed onto the wolf's back and the wolf led him up tiny mountain paths. Everything had become cooler and quieter. Jumping Mouse felt the breeze on his whiskers, and the air tasted of the purest snow.

Sounds were sharp and clear. They anchored themselves deep inside his mouse-heart. Then at the top of the mountains the wolf said: 'We are here now, Jumping Mouse. I will take you to the edge of a mountain lake and leave you there.'

When they arrived at the lake Jumping Mouse said, 'Describe this place to me.' The wolf tried. He described how the mountains were huge, with purple tips and how the tips poked through the mists, and how everything was calm and peaceful.

'I could spend eternity giving you the details,' said the wolf, 'but the details alone are quite irrelevant.'

Jumping Mouse spent the night on the mountain. Next morning he felt his way to the edge of the lake and dipped his paw into the water. When he drank from the lake it tasted so clear and fresh that he knew immediately it was the source of the Great River. 'I have arrived at its beginning,' he marvelled.

There was no shelter at all now, and no other creatures were likely to come to his aid in so isolated a place. Jumping Mouse did not care. He sat alone by the edge of the lake and listened to drifting sounds. He smelt and touched the grass. Everything was peaceful, everything was good. He thought of things he had never thought about before, and he realised he did not wish to be back among the tree-roots ever again. He felt as if he had reached the end of one journey and the beginning of another.

And then in the middle of his back Jumping Mouse felt an odd sensation, and up above he heard the noise an eagle makes. One was coming for him now. He felt the rush of wind as huge wings came down from the sky and a great bird descended on him. He was terrified as he felt its claws grab round his body, and then he did not mind at all. He felt himself being lifted from the ground. Up and up he went, higher and higher.

And up above he heard the noise an eagle makes.

Out on the Great Plain he saw the buffalo thundering along.

The next thing he knew, he was beginning to see again. He saw colours and shapes. Everything seemed crystal clear, and all the time he was rising higher and higher. He laughed! Oh, he was sure he had wings! He was sure he could fly! It was a wonderful feeling! This rush of the wind! This perfect freedom! He felt that, like the eagle, he had a beak, and claws and perfect sight.

Everything was clearer than he had thought possible. He saw the tree in whose roots he had once lived, and among the roots he saw the mice, still working and moving their seeds from one place to another. Nearby he saw the raccoon, then the wolf, and out on the Great Plain he saw the buffalo thundering along. And there was the frog by the Great River! Jumping Mouse felt so happy and free.

He shouted down to his friend the frog, and his voice seemed changed.
'Hello, Brother Frog,' he called, all the time rising higher and higher.
And the frog looked up from the river and shouted, 'Hello, Brother Eagle.'

OTHER BOOKS FROM HAWTHORN PRESS

Pancakes for Findus

Sven Nordqvist

A Sunday Times children's book of the week

This is the first story in the adventures of farmer Pettson and his cat Findus. Pettson wants to bake a birthday cake for the cat who has three birthdays a year. But how can they get the eggs when the bull is in the way?

Findus and Pettson live in a ramshackle cottage in the country, with a henhouse, workshop and woodshed. Their world is a fascinating, magical one inhabited by tiny creatures who move Pettson's things about when he isn't looking.

Sven Nordqvist is a leading Swedish children's illustrator and writer. The Findus and Pettson stories draw on his playful adventures with his two young sons. His unique illustrations are inspired by a delight in everyday life.

'Lively, silly, a cross between Wallace and Gromit and a European folk-tale – this is pure good fun.'
NZ Listener

Findus and Pettson Series
Illustrated with full colour line drawings throughout   28pp; 297 × 210mm
Hardback; ISBN 978-1-903458-79-2

£10.99

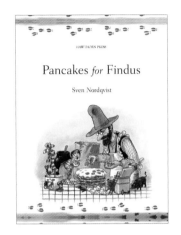

When Findus was Little and Disappeared

Sven Nordqvist

Farmer Pettson sat doing the crossword, with Findus the cat on his knee. "Tell me about when I disappeared," said Findus. "You haven't disappeared," said Pettson, "you're sitting right here." "Yes, but – when I was little." "Oh then ... But you've heard the story so often before." "But tell it to me anyway!" So here is the story of when Findus was little and disappeared.

"I can't recommend them highly enough. Hurrah for Findus!"
Philip Pullman

Findus and Pettson Series
Illustrated with full colour line drawings throughout   28pp; 297 × 210mm
Hardback; ISBN 978-1-903458-83-9

£10.99

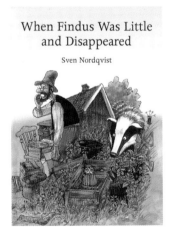

Findus and the Fox

Sven Nordqvist

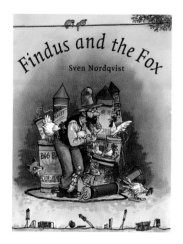

There's a hen-hunting fox on the loose. But farmer Pettson and his quirky cat Findus agree that foxes shouldn't be killed. They should be tricked. They come up with a fabulous plan, which makes for an explosive, unforgettable night.

'It's not often that we come across books with such immediate and lasting appeal as Sven Nordqvist's Findus books. The stories are ingenious, the characters are quirky and original, and the illustrations are absolutely delightful.   Philip Pullman

Findus and Pettson Series
Illustrated with full colour line drawings throughout   28pp; 297 × 210mm
Hardback; ISBN 978-1-903458-87-7

£10.99

Findus goes Camping

Sven Nordqvist

Findus and Pettson live in a red farmhouse, with a henhouse, workshop and toolshed set among forests, fields and meadows.

One day, Findus finds a tent in the attic. Pettson starts imagining how it will be going camping by the lake, catching fish and grilling them over the fire as the sun sets. This is not exactly how things turn out, as Findus, Pettson and the hens try hiking – in the garden.

'I've seldom seen such an endless, apparently effortless flow of invention. Readers young and old will spend happy hours poring over them to find all the details, and revisit them again and again.   Philip Pullman

Findus and Pettson Series
Publication 1 April 2010
Illustrated with full colour line drawings throughout   28pp; 297 × 210 mm
Hardback; ISBN 978-1-903458-91-4

£10.99

All the Dear Little Animals

Ulf Nilsson, illustrated by Eva Eriksson

Three children decide someone must bury all the world's poor dead animals. 'The whole world is full of dead things,' said Esther. 'In every bush there is a bird, a butterfly, a mouse. Someone must be kind and look after them. Someone must make a sacrifice and see that all these things are buried.' 'Who must?' I asked. 'We must,' she said.

This is a picture book for children aged five and up, and covers a difficult subject in an unsentimental way. It describes exactly the way children resolve big issues – through play. It was chosen by Swedish children as one of their favourite books in 2008. Eva Eriksson is one of Sweden's best-loved children's illustrators, winning the Astrid Lindgren and prestigious August prizes.

'This captivating book takes us on a safe, funny and deeply meaningful adventure.'
Julie Stokes OBE, Founder and Clinical Director of Winston's Wish

'The best book I have seen perhaps in years. I just love it'   Kate de Goldi, NZ National Radio

Illustrated in colour, with apple green endpapers   32pp; 210 × 218mm
Hardback; ISBN 978-1-903458-94-5
£9.99

Goodbye Mr Muffin

Ulf Nilsson, illustrated by Anna-Clara Tidholm

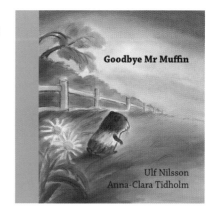

In his youth, Mr Muffin was a strong guinea pig who could carry a whole cucumber on his back. Now old, grey and tired, he looks back on his life. Then one Wednesday morning, he feels a sharp pain in his stomach ...

This picture book is for ages three and up. It tells the touching story about the death of a much-loved pet. Growing old, death rites, the question of the afterlife, all are handled with warmth and gentle humour. *Goodbye Mr Muffin* won the 2002 Swedish August Prize.

Anna-Clara Tidholm is winner of numerous awards. Ulf Nilsson is a celebrated Swedish author, who has won the August and US Batchelder prizes.

Children's Classics   Publication 1 March 2010
Illustrated in colour   44pp; 210 × 218mm
Hardback; ISBN 978-1-903458-36-5
£9.99

Ordering books

If you have difficulties ordering Hawthorn Press books from a bookshop, you can order direct from:

United Kingdom

Booksource
50 Cambuslang Road
Glasgow, G32 8NB
Tel: (0845) 370 0063
Fax: (0845) 370 0064
E-mail: orders@booksource.net

USA/North America

Steiner Books
PO Box 960, Herndon
VA 20172-0960
Tel: (800) 856 8664
Fax: (703) 661 1501
E-mail: service@steinerbooks.org
Website: www.steinerbooks.org

or you can order online at **www.hawthornpress.com**

For further information or a book catalogue, please contact:

Hawthorn Press
1 Lansdown Lane, Stroud
Gloucestershire GL5 1BJ
Tel: (01453) 757040
Fax: (01453) 751138
E-mail: info@hawthornpress.com
Website: www.hawthornpress.com